The Girl Who Was Convinced Beyond All Reason that She Could Fly

SYBIL
LAMB

ARSENAL PULP PRESS
VANCOUVER

THE GIRL WHO WAS CONVINCED BEYOND ALL REASON THAT SHE COULD FLY
Copyright © 2020 by Sybil Lamb

ARSENAL PULP PRESS
Suite 202 – 211 East Georgia St.
Vancouver, BC V6A 1Z6
Canada
arsenalpulp.com

The publisher gratefully acknowledges the support of the Canada Council for the Arts and the British Columbia Arts Council for its publishing program, and the Government of Canada, and the Government of British Columbia (through the Book Publishing Tax Credit Program), for its publishing activities.

Arsenal Pulp Press acknowledges the xʷməθkʷəy̓əm (Musqueam), Sḵwx̱wú7mesh (Squamish), and səlilwətaɬ (Tsleil-Waututh) Nations, custodians of the traditional, ancestral, and unceded territories where our office is located. We pay respect to their histories, traditions, and continuous living cultures and commit to accountability, respectful relations, and friendship.

This is a work of fiction. Any resemblance of characters to persons either living or deceased is purely coincidental.

Cover illustrations by Sybil Lamb
Cover and text design by Jazmin Welch
Edited by Shirarose Wilensky
Proofread by Alison Strobel

Printed and bound in Canada

Library and Archives Canada Cataloguing in Publication:
Title: The girl who was convinced beyond all reason that she could fly / Sybil Lamb.
Names: Lamb, Sybil, 1975– author.
Identifiers: Canadiana (print) 20200202723 | Canadiana (ebook) 20200202731 |
    ISBN 9781551528175 (softcover) | ISBN 9781551528182 (HTML)
Classification: LCC PS8623.A48265 G57 2020 | DDC jC813/.6—dc23

Dedicated to

Squeaky & Twitchy.

Plunder every highway of all the chili cheese 4evr.

♥

You can't park here.

CONTENTS

1

THE GIRL WHO WAS
NOT A BIRD

This one time there was a girl who was convinced beyond all reason that she could fly.

She was shy and bold at the same time. No one knew where she came from. She mostly kept to herself, but she was always nearby, perched on roofs and fire escapes. If you caught a glimpse of her bouncing around in the air, you would probably squint and rub your eyes and think you got confused.

The first person to talk to her was Grackle McCart. Grack had a bicycle hot dog cart with the longest menu in town. Everybody loved him because he had every kind of hot dog—100 of them, in fact—seriously every kind, like tofu, turkey, tongue, and even toffee and tamarind.

Grack himself? He was just super chill, smart, silly, and charming. He was dorky in a cool way and cool in a dorky way. He'd always be pedalling his hot dog cart around the market, smiling, and then if he caught your eye he'd go, "Hungry? Good thing I got here in time," and then wink at you.

Shopkeepers and cashiers flagged him down all day for hot dogs: he'd sell them to the pet store and the Popsicle store and the broken electronics store and the scissors store and the misprinted T-shirt shop. Afterward, the loud, crazy punk rockers and art weirdos from the notorious trash-strewn five-dollar hotel would try to talk cheap hot dogs out of him all night.

Running a hot dog cart meant he was parked on the same corners for hours. Grack spent oodles of time watching the busy market streets, scanning for hungry hot dog buyers. So he noticed small details all the time.

Then came the day. Grack was refilling the ghost pepper chipotle mayo when he looked up and saw—he was pretty sure?—a girl jumping back and forth between the three-storey brick buildings. It was surely an unjumpable distance. There were two lanes of traffic and rows of parked cars, and a bunch of shuffling pedestrians too busy shopping or lugging giant boxes to notice.

The next day, it was a slow afternoon, and Grack was cleaning his grill and throwing stale hot dog buns to the pigeons. Out of nowhere a feral-eyed girl jumped down off the fire escape behind him, grabbed a bun out of the air, and landed atop a mailbox, all without touching the ground.

Grack's mind was blown. But as the youngest son of the biggest hot dog family in town, he had seen all kinds of crazy things, so he played it cool.

"What kind of bird are you?" he asked the girl.

She looked thoughtful while chewing her mouthful of hot dog bun, then said bashfully, "I'm not a bird, I'm just a regular flying girl."

She stuffed the rest of the hot dog bun into her cheeks and scrambled up the fire escape. When she got to the top, she kept climbing up into the air and disappeared.

Grackle McCart was in awe and kind of smitten.

Ever after, the flying girl would roost on the phone poles and window ledges and fire escapes by Grack's hot dog cart. When no one was buying hot dogs, Grack would look up and search all the roofs and window-sills for the girl who seemed convinced that she could fly. Sometimes she'd bounce from the roof on one side of the street to the other. Other times he'd see her almost hidden next to an air conditioner or nestled in the awning of a shop.

One day, Grack honked his two AHOOGAH horns and rang his three bike bells until she looked his way. Then he made his cool-guy-eyebrows move and grinned.

"Hey, I got too many hot dogs again this afternoon. Help me eat a few?" He said the first thing he could think of to get this weird, wild girl to hang out with a regular, nerdy hot dog guy like him.

To his delight, she chirped, "Okay!" and launched-fell off the nearest roof, bounced off a store awning, floated over a parked car, and landed in a gleeful crouch on top of the closest trash can. She was all a jumble of motion that seemed like the routine of a clumsy, careless trapeze artist, except she didn't have any ropes.

Without discussion, the girl and Grack decided they should probably hang out every day from now on.

The girl would drop out of the sky and stick around for brunch, lunch, snacks, and dinner. At first, they never talked about themselves. The girl would tell him about stuff she'd seen from up high, like a giant hats-and-guitars party in the courtyard of the burrito place, or the glow-in-the-dark Frisbee she'd found atop the ice cream shop. Grack would gossip about how he'd made hot dogs for a bunch of hip-hop stars and some big-deal sports guys, plus he knew a place with free video games as long as you kept buying milkshakes.

He invited her to check out the video game milk-shake place maybe? But she said she wasn't really great with the indoors, and Grack didn't argue 'cause he didn't want to leave his hot dog bike alone for long anyways.

And then someone would come along for a hot dog and the girl would tumble sideways up the nearest building like a tumbleweed that made a ninety-degree wrong turn.

2

THE WEIRDLY
SPECIFIC MARKET

The Weirdly Specific Market always had people coming and going, buying weirdly specific stuff at the market's weirdly specific stores. Shoppers came to buy enough T-shirts to fill a whole truck or a new set of number buttons for their elevator. Or they went to the strange, dark underground club for eating cheese and looking at pictures. One store only sold bolts and screws, and one store only sold empty takeout containers. There was a specialty shoe–boot place that converted shoes into boots and vice versa. One store was made entirely of rooms of milk crates filled with stereo cables in an old, abandoned department store. The point was: everybody needs some kind of weirdly specific thing at some point. When they did, they came to the market.

The market also had dozens of butchers, cheesers, and bakers. There was a grocer that sold rare, fancy purple and blue apples, and one where you could get a bag of 1,000 carrots for twenty bucks. There were dozens of ice cream and hot snack carts, and Grack? Well, he was the most popular one, thanks to his Infamous 100 Hot Dog Menu.

Since Grack had been running a hot dog cart since before he could read, he had the experience to cleverly figure out that most people would stop and hang out, waiting to see what happens, if, say, they saw some bananas hijinks like a shoeless girl endangering herself by climbing up and jumping off roofs and street lamps and phone poles. Then, once she didn't actually smash herself into the ground but instead kept on fluttering about like a featherless bird, most people would eventually look down and see the Infamous 100 Hot Dog Menu, which was carefully designed so at least one dog appealed to someone's particular vice, craving, or guilty pleasure.

With the girl who wasn't a bird around, people walked past Grack's cart at half speed and then got even slower.

19

His business doubled and kept increasing. Before long, regulars at the market had started saying stuff like:

"Hey, let's get hot dogs from that crazy bike cart with like 100 different kinds of dog. There's a girl who's always there and she was probably born and raised in a travelling circus, then abandoned here a few summers ago and adopted by pigeons. She hangs out on top of the traffic light and will jump off it and catch french fries in mid-air. One time, a guy bet her a corn dog that she couldn't hop, skip, and jump herself to the top of the market water tower, so she took his hat and bounced crazily and carelessly twenty metres up the tower and almost plummeted onto the cement sidewalk a bunch of times. But then she stuck the hat on top like the water tower was wearing it. It's still up there!"

All the nearby punk rockers from the five-dollars-a-night hotel started called the girl Eggs after her one and only T-shirt that she always wore, all faded and torn up. It read, *EGGS*, and it was from a TV commercial recommending people eat two servings of eggs daily. She loved that shirt so much that if you tried to tell her chickens can't fly, she'd just climb up the closest wall away from you.

3

CAN A GIRL FLY?

All day and every day Eggs would fly around town aimlessly fluttering. She'd appear not long after the sun came up and disappear just after it went down. (Flying at night, she once mentioned, causes ten times as many crashes as during the day.) She would get all over town most days. She claimed to really like the roofs of the food carts at the mall 'cause people would let her finish their fries all the time, and she could fly to the drive-in next door and see movies but without the sound. Afterward, she would go back to the food cart roofs and listen to people who'd just been at the drive-in talk about the movie.

Two of the hotel punks told Grack they had seen Eggs at the amusement park a week ago. She had been riding the roller coaster but the opposite way to everyone else. She'd flutter all over the tallest parts of the roller coaster, and then when the coaster train cars with people in them came by, she'd jump-fall off the track and flip and land on the next ride. For this she got in mega trouble with amusement park security, who chased her around for an hour with a giant butterfly net. The guards said they'd put her in a giant birdcage if she came to the park again, but the joke was on them 'cause by then she'd already been on all the rides.

Once, Grack couldn't help but kind of sort of ask her: "How do you do it? How can anybody move around in the air like that?"

Eggs had made a grave, serious face, like she was gently breaking bad news. She said she couldn't remember a time she didn't fly. In her earliest memories, she wanted to be everywhere. See everything. And always keep going up and up and up and up.

She said, "Flying is my favourite thing in the world. When you fly, you never want for anything, but you get to see everything. A bird's-eye view of stuff everyone thought no one could see. The city becomes a big unfolded map of itself, and you can see how the world fits together. You can see how everything works. When you get in trouble, nothing bad happens because you can get away fast and you're almost impossible to catch."

She explained that most people can't fly because of a common misunderstanding of how flying works.

"Most people imagine flying is done by falling sideways instead of down. This is precisely right but also totally mixed up and wrong. Yes, that is what flying *is*," Eggs said, "but it is not how it works! People mistakenly think they're supposed to fall and then just forget to hit the ground. But then they focus on trying not to fall, instead of on doing flying stuff."

Grack laughed and said, "Yeah, yeah, yeah, I know exactly what you're talking about."

He actually had no idea what she was talking about, but it wasn't reeeeeeally a lie. He was always pretty sure he was on the verge of being able to understand her. At the very least, he really liked her and thought being friends with her was the coolest. Grack was Eggs's best friend pretty much, and no one else spent much time hanging out with her, so that must mean he

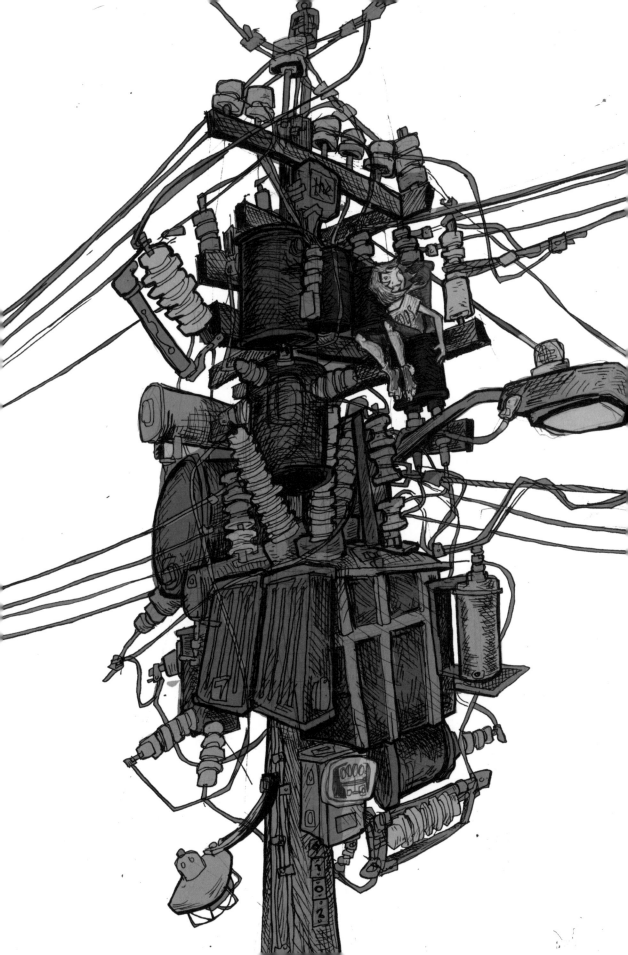

understood her, right? And, logically, that must mean he understood what the girl had just told him.

Grack decided basically that Eggs had superpowers. Like a superhero but more realistic and hard-won. In Grack's mind, a superhero who was also basically a regular girl was more possible than a flying girl.

Undeniable was the fact that she did possess a superhuman climbing ability. She could scurry up to any roof in seconds. She would flutter up a feature-less brick wall with an ease powered only by her own belief that she was flying. The other half of her con-viction that she could fly was 'cause she had jumped off more than 100 buildings and not died once. Her record flight would be a leap off a fourteen-storey building, even though she was utterly un-aerodynamic-looking. She was just a little bit taller than a short person, with a bit of a tummy from Grack giving her unlimited hot dogs.

Grack said the dogs were just in exchange for Eggs flying around the neighbourhood for him flyering for his hot dog cart. But really, he felt so proud and special that this new, strange, amazing girl liked him. And he wouldn't let her eat his trash, even if she dove off a building to grab it out of the air.

Eggs could balance teetering on chimneys and phone wires with a dumb luck more powerful than any practised skill, flinging flyers at passersby below with okayish accuracy. And when she ran out, she'd climb as high as she could and stretch upward, testing the air, flapping human arms that were neither strong nor skinny, threatening to launch herself into the sky, if she ever found the wind she was waiting for.

So, that was Eggs, the girl who was convinced beyond all reason that she could fly. Mostly harmless, kind of cute, sweet, and funny, and, if nothing else, possibly the luckiest nut on the roof.

Everyone let her get away with everything, including believing that she flew. We all wished it were true. She was like a fairy-tale superhero, but she was real, and we could say we knew her.

4

THE GROUND
IS HOT LAVA

Eggs seemed to live nowhere.

If anyone asked, Eggs usually claimed she lived in the bird feeder at the tiny park next to an old mushroom and root vegetable market. Everyone knew that couldn't be true, but no one wanted to call her on it.

Grack would start pedalling his cart around at dawn, selling his bacon, sausage, and hash brown–bun dogs, to catch people on their way to work. Eggs would appear before any of the half-awake shopkeepers had

even gone for coffee, so nobody noticed her groggily hanging off a street lamp, looking more like a bat than a bird.

One time, a woman buying a party-size bag of fish hot dogs told Grack that she had been getting her braces tightened at an orthodontist up on the sixth floor of the tallest building on the edge of the market, and mayyyybe it had been the Novocaine, but she thought she'd seen the flying girl sleeping between the air conditioners on the roof of the wholesale coffee mug warehouse.

Grack was pretty sure that Eggs was living behind the sign of the old department store full of milk crates of stereo cables. It was a giant old metal sign that said *DEPARTMENT STORE* in big red neon letters and had 992 burnt-out light bulbs and eight flickering ones that worked. It had wires and pigeons all over it. He wondered if Eggs got along with birds, how they negotiated who got to nest where.

The truth was, sometimes Eggs fell asleep balanced on top of a phone pole in sight of Grack's hot dog cart. She'd tried sleeping in trees at the amusement park a bunch of times, but the security guys with the giant butterfly net were increasingly on her case every week. She definitely didn't want to stay at the five-dollar punk hotel, even in the discount room on the roof. The whole place was just punks trying to talk the loudest and breaking things 24-7. Oh, sure, they ate lots of hot dogs and were mostly all chill and funny, but any random misinterpreted comment could lead to dozens of punk boys and girls stomping in circles and breaking TVs while screaming made-up songs and then setting a chair on fire. Eggs thought it was a nice place to visit but an impossible place to sleep.

Grack was getting frustrated they only hung out while he was working, even if he did kinda work from dawn to dusk with no days off. He wanted to just hang out for real, so one day he tried to tempt Eggs back to his apartment with the promise of a whole box of melt-proof ice cream sandwiches he got by mistake and therefore needed her help eating.

Eggs followed Grack home, bouncing along the street lamps and no-parking signs until Grack rode his bicycle hot dog cart into an old boxy stone building. The open door looked at least 100 years old, from a time they would have parked horse-drawn stuff in there.

But instead of carriages and wagons, inside there were rows of food carts, both motorized and pedal-powered. They ranged in size from a little tricycle with two buckets for ice cream to a bell-and-whistle-covered school bus wienermobile with an all-stainless-steel mobile kitchen grill. The warehouse-sized room even had four separate walk-in coolers, holding enough meat, veggies, buns, and fixin's to feed a full baseball stadium for a month.

Eggs flutter-wriggled under the stone arch of the big door, then fluttered regularly across the metal beams of the ceiling.

She was surprised and impressed. "Wow, hot dog bicycles must make a lot of money," she said, kind of like a half question.

Grack beamed proudly. "Yes, they do," he said, and then grinned at her and did his cool-guy eyebrows.

The carts and trucks and stuff weren't all specifically his. This building and everything in it was the family business. Aunts, uncles, grandparents, great-grandparents, and their brothers and sisters and all that—more family than he could count—lived in this building, and everyone had their own hot dog cart.

Grack turned to Eggs, who was dangling from a support beam. He took off his glasses, looked her in the eye, and said: "I am Grackle McCart, and you are standing in the McCart family hot dog empire built by over 100 years of hot dog sales. My great-great-grandfather Elijah Snipe McCart is the original inventor of the hot dog cart. I am the youngest heir to the McCart Empire, and I am inviting you into it."

"What are you talking about?" Eggs said.

She was confused about what the heck was going on and felt afraid and confused from all this being indoors. She tried to jump out a window to clear her head, but embarrassingly, she mistook a clean window for an open one and slammed into it face-first. Stunned, she fell on her butt on the garage floor.

"Welcome to Earth," said Grack. It was the first time he'd ever seen her actually land. He motioned for her to follow him down the cold dark stone staircase that went underground. "I'm talking about you pedalling one of these carts. We could work the market and do my route in opposite directions. Forget working for hot dogs—you could have *money*, Eggs."

Eggs shook her head, confused and in pain. Then she looked down and realized she was on the ground.

She started to panic, as if she had seen herself on fire or getting eaten by sharks. With an explosion of energy, she spun her arms and legs wildly, scrambling to get off the floor as fast as she could. She very seriously acted like the floor was made of red-hot lava. Delirious, she managed to claw her way on top of an old BBQ bicycle cart, messily knocking several buckets of corn relish and hot peppers off the cart's fixin's shelf and sloppily spilling them all down the side.

"I can't sell stuff! I don't know how! I just like watching you do it and helping," she blurted. She was getting more and more agitated. "I promise I'll clean that mess up. Why are we in this giant garage?"

"Don't worry about cleaning it up!" Grack said. "Come down to my apartment, and you can clean yourself up."

Since he was the youngest McCart, Grack lived in the basement with his three older sisters and two cousins and a few dogs. The first floor was for his three older brothers and his mom, the second floor was for his aunts and uncles, all the way up to his super-old great-uncle on the top floor.

"Living with tons of family isn't bad at all," Grack told Eggs. "My apartment is actually pretty big and you absolutely *have* to see my awesome all-steel kitchen. The two of us could cook stuff I don't even have in my cart! Like sandwiches maybe, or how about roast chicken? Or what if we baked a cake together? With all of my family's food cart supplies, we could make literally anything you could ever want to eat!"

But Eggs, still completely panicking about touching the ground, wasn't listening. She climbed up the wall again and was clattering her fingers on the window over and over, like she was trying to dig through it.

"I WON'T GO ON THE GROUND AND I DEFINITELY WON'T GO IN THE GROUND," she bleated.

Grack pleaded for her to listen to his reasonable reasons. He promised she'd learn how to do money and sales, like his sisters and brothers. And he promised to teach her everything he knew about cooking,

not just working the grill and deep fryer but fancy chef stuff, too. If nothing else, she at least had to check out his room? He had a cool rare music collection and some movies and his own mini fridge with every kind of cola and a goofy, fun pet dog he'd named Bunny 'cause he ate carrots and could do jumping tricks.

He said, "I have a postcard collection and a foreign coin collection and two goldfish, and I really do have that whole box of ice cream sandwiches. I have a spare bicycle that you could use, and we could ride bikes together—if you can ride a bike?" Grack thought Eggs must be able to ride a bike if she can stand on a phone wire for hours every day. With her powers, she could probably instantly master all the bike tricks there are ...

What Grack was trying to say was that he'd give Eggs anything if it made her hang out with him more.

But Eggs was still clawing at the window, with her toes locked in a white-knuckle grip on the old brick wall.

Then Grack lost it. She was supposed to hang out at his house! Grack would be in big trouble with his dad if he found Eggs in the garage, and she was hardly listening to him while he tried to think of anything to impress her. He felt hurt and insulted, like Eggs was acting extra weird so she wouldn't have to talk normal with him.

"Why can't you get your head out of the clouds?" Grack snapped. "Why do you have to be such a bird-brain?!" His voice carried as much angry meanness as he could muster.

Eggs started to cry, making sounds like the ugly squawk of a seagull. She finally fumbled the window open and shot out so fast she was a block away by the time Grack could poke his head out to look for her.

5

SPLENDID FAIRY WREN'S SPACE BOOK

Eggs skittered to the top of Grack's building, where she launched herself from rooftop to rooftop in random directions. Direction was of no importance as long as she kept getting farther away. The old brick and stone buildings of the market faded into the cement, barnwood, and steel of the mill district.

Then she found herself surrounded by odd lumpy buildings with not enough windows and more exterior pipes and ductwork than could possibly be usable. The lumpy buildings went for blocks in every direction.

Eventually, she flew between two rows of tall concrete silos, then disappeared into a clutter of old textile mills cut up and repurposed as tiny apartments. Eggs was suddenly charmed by the rickety, cobbled-together buildings. They were connected by narrow courtyards, and it made for a fascinating place to fly.

It was no secret that Eggs delighted in sneaking into places. She never got in trouble because she was more harmless than an actual bird. She wouldn't put anything in her pockets because she refused to take on extra weight.

The local bad guys had long ago given up trying to recruit her into their dumb bad-guy gang. She was utterly disqualified as a cat burglar, or even as an egg burglar.

Tonight, her airheaded harmlessness was charmingly apparent as she tumbled into the tiny triangular attic room of Splendid Fairy Wren.

Splendid Fairy Wren was a semi-grown-up punk rocker who was also really a hippie. She had left the five-dollar punk hotel a year ago to move into this tiny room, which she paid for by knitting socks for a buck a pair. She had picked the highest room in town on purpose, so she could hide and knit and read books and grow plants in old cans.

Eggs had chosen this window because it was the highest and looked like a challenge. She crashed through a dozen of Splendid Wren's plants on the window ledge. Eggs dangled upside down from the sill and almost caught every single plant she'd knocked over.

Wren smiled uncertainly up from a big picture book about outer space. "Oh, hey," she said, trying to

hide the confusion in her voice. Splendid Wren figured that maybe she was supposed to know a flying girl would crash through her window tonight and she'd better pretend she remembered.

"Heya!" Eggs smiled big and upside downly.

Splendid Wren seemed friendly but was also super anxious about her plants. "Hey, you knocked over one of my cacti! She has to get back in her little pot or she'll turn into a sad little spiky raisin."

Eggs apologized repeatedly and nervously. She volunteered to clean up the mess she'd made.

"Actually, I fly everywhere all the time, but I don't always fly in such complicated, cluttered building mazes," Eggs humblebragged, and in the same breath despaired, "so technically, as a flying girl who spends most of her time flying, I have no idea how to garden or anything to do with the ground, but I still want to do the right thing and help."

Wren pointed at the uprooted cactus on the floor. "I would rather do the gardening myself, but you can pick up the cactus and place it in the can while I spoon in the dirt."

Eggs overeagerly and overconfidently grabbed the cactus, and then immediately dropped it again, squawking in pain from the spikes.

Wren laughed and gave Eggs some Band-Aids, and they promptly decided to be friends.

Eggs wound up hanging out at Splendid Wren's all night. They replanted the cactus, and Wren excitedly told Eggs the names of all her plants and which ones she thought were dating and which ones she thought didn't like each other. She even had special unusual plants like a teeny-tiny apple tree growing in a coffee cup. Eggs didn't see any apples, but Wren said they were too small to see. Then she showed Eggs the two dozen different kinds of socks she could knit, including pom-pom heels, stripy, polka-dot, argyle, Xtreme cold cable-knit, and rainbow toe socks.

Splendid Wren was wound up like a triple-size rubber band, so grateful for company after her year of self-imposed hermitting. With contagious bubbling mirth, she continued to show Eggs around her place, starting with her well-worn pile of picture books. They were all weirdly specific because she had bought them at the Weirdly Specific Market: books like *The Fish of the*

Southern Hemisphere, *Post Office Airplanes*, *250 Years of Robots*, and *Garbage Cans of the World*. And Wren had made up backstories for every single picture in every single book.

"Say," said Wren suddenly, "it's just about time for pancakes!"

Wren had a huge sack of pancake mix, as it was her favourite food and the only thing she ever ate. (Sometimes she'd snip one of her flowers and put petals in the pancakes.) Eggs could stay all night and hang out in Wren's giant understuffed beanbag chair, as it was her only piece of actual furniture. And they could eat pancakes and look at pictures of planets and fish!

Eggs thought Wren was indeed splendid. Her silly playfulness was a delightful and much-needed change from most non-flying people. When you're the only one who flies, limits the number of fun things you can do with other kids. And Eggs's talent for gravity (or problem, depending on your point of view) had always coloured her ability to make and keep friends.

Eggs's only topic of conversation was all the cool, weird things she'd seen while flying. Like chickens and goats in people's backyards, and boats hidden on their roofs for the off-season. She'd seen secret terraces, secret radio stations, secret flying-machine landing pads, and all kinds of giant contraptions, rooftop greenhouses, and messy private patios on high ledges.

And she'd seen all the curious people in strange apartments. So many people think no one can see through their windows because they're high up. There are people who live in piles of cats and dogs, and people who live in piles of pizza boxes and newspapers. There are poor people with luxury houses and rich people who treat their condos like barns. Eggs could list off strange characters for hours without stopping—and she did, until Wren fell asleep.

The whole time, Eggs balanced on top of Wren's refrigerator, refusing to touch the ground, even fourteen floors up.

6

FOURTEEN FLOORS IN FORTY-TWO SECONDS

The next morning, Eggs snapped awake with the sun. She stretched and fluttered to the window ledge, announcing that she would fly away now.

Splendid Wren pleaded with Eggs, "Just let me make you some tea—or maybe some eggs, if that's not weird—and then maybe stay and live with me forever?"

But before Wren could finish her racing words, Eggs disappeared. She plummeted out the window while Wren was mumbling, "See you later ..."

Wren stared uncertainly at the empty window, her brain a tangled mess of dropped stitches. Had the most unusual girl she'd ever met just flown in her window, told her all kinds of impossible stories, and then flown out again? Or had Wren been alone so long she was seeing things?

Now that Eggs was gone, Wren wasn't sure if she'd been real or a waking dream, or maybe Wren was still dreaming. Maybe she'd had one of those flying dreams that dream doctors are always talking about.

Wren was mostly sure Eggs was real and had probably just flown off to go sit on a statue or get some worms or something. "That's just what flying girls must be like," Wren reasoned to herself.

She opened up a secret box of cookies and lined three of them along the window ledge, carefully positioning them so they could be noticed from a

few metres away in any direction. Then she flopped into her beanbag chair and picked up her space book where she'd left off. So lost was Wren in her thoughts, she didn't think to run to the window to see where Eggs had gone after that fourteen-storey drop.

Eggs's dawn flight out the fourteenth-floor window took a spectacular forty-two seconds. She hit everything possible on the way down. Eggs plinkety-plonked down through the random outcroppings, bouncing every which way, ricocheting off phone wires and clotheslines, deflecting off a fire escape with a mortally perilous CLANG, and propelling herself forward and sometimes upward by randomly pinwheeling her limbs. The alleys, shafts, and court-yards of the mill apartments were just as jagged and maze-like as the buildings they belonged to. In 100 completely unalike rooms, apartment dwellers were waking up and sipping coffee and chewing on toast, gazing out their windows, when a live thrashing girl shot noisily past. Everyone blinked and rubbed their eyes and involuntarily yawned. They presumed they must still be more than half-asleep.

In the end, Eggs landed in a tree. She was covered in scratches and bruises but otherwise absurdly unharmed. Exhausted from her pinball-machine tumble, she hung out in the tree for hours, watching the tiny odd-shaped apartment dwellers straggle off to their jobs ten feet below.

Eggs had certainly messed herself up way worse a bunch of times. She'd even broken both arms, each on a different flight. So many times, it seemed like Eggs had finally used up her impossible luck. Someone would find her smashed-up body crumpled over a parked car or a mailbox and drag her to the hospital, and it'd seem like that was it for old Eggs. But she healed inhumanly fast every time. She would leave the hospital by the window.

No one even noticed when Eggs disappeared from the tree in time for lunch.

7

NO MORE HOT DOGS

When Eggs reappeared at Grack's cart, asking to distribute flyers in exchange for free hot dogs again, he said, "No. No way. I don't need any flighty bird girl taking advantage of me like I'm a dumb sucker."

Several boys and a couple of girls whose houses she'd broken into had *major* crushes on Eggs. They were always poking around trying to find her. Grackle McCart knew that. He couldn't help being a little bit jealous.

Eggs was surprised. "But, but, I only ate so many hot dogs 'cause I thought you liked that I ate any kind of hot dog you cooked," she said. "I didn't know you wanted to sell those. I thought I was just eating the spare hot dogs."

Grack could see that Eggs really didn't understand, and that just made

him more upset. What, was he supposed to *not* get upset with her just 'cause she was a wild animal? Or because she thought she was a wild animal, or wanted to pretend she was a wild animal, or whatever?

He stared hard at her perched on top of a parking meter. "I heard you spent the night at Splendid Wren's. But you wouldn't even take one step down the stone stairs into my place," he said. "I should have known anyone pretending to be a bird would make a pretend friend."

Grack scrunched up his face because he didn't want to cry in front of her.

Eggs got sad. She didn't understand why Grack was upset. He was her closest friend. He fed her and he kinda took care of her.

Grack just stayed hunched over his grill, cooking fish-stick-sized hot dogs. He wanted her to apologize, or maybe tell him she liked him best? Or ... he didn't know what. "I don't know what to think," he sulked.

Eggs got all jittery and started asking dumb questions too fast. She kept saying she would do flyers and he didn't even have to give her any snacks and it's all cool.

"No, it's not cool," he said. He told her she had the day off and tomorrow too and don't call him and he'd find her if he decided he needed flyering by carrier pigeon again but probably not.

Grack wanted her to go away soon because he couldn't make himself not cry for much longer. And he could tell that Eggs was also trying not to have feelings inside of herself.

"No, for real. Go on, get out of here," he said. "Go break into somebody else's house or whatever." And then he picked up an undercooked corn dog and threw it spinning down the length of the block. "Why don't you do a cool trick and disappear?"

Eggs's eyes looked hurt, but her mouth was a single expressionless line. "It's my life to fly around and fly away," she told him. "It's been my life for longer than I can remember."

And with that, she fluttered up the nearest fire escape and disappeared.

Hours later, the very second that the sunset touched the horizon, Splendid Fairy Wren appeared next to Grackle McCart. Grack remembered her from when she'd lived at the punk hotel. She was dressed in a tangled pile of unfinished knitted sweaters with her head wrapped in extra-long scarves, lugging a coarse burlap sack of hammers and rusty tools.

The overdressed Wren said, "I've come outside for the longest time in a year specifically to see you, because I know you are closer to Eggs than anybody."

Grack was half-delighted, half-suspicious. "Does Eggs really talk about me and stuff?"

"She thinks you're the biggest deal in town!" Wren said. "Running your hot dog stand and giving her food and jobs to do and always knowing stuff. Tons of people go to your hot dog cart every day. She's in awe of you because, since she landed here, you're the first and most consistent friend she's had. She said a bunch of times that without you she'd have wound up a freaky garbage bird roosting under the highway off-ramp."

Grack's heart did a backflip, but he tried to play it cool. He said, "I thought Eggs just slept at your place now."

"Kind of," said Wren. "She nodded off on top of my fridge. But she never laid down, or even sat. Anyway, would you help me build her a house?" She reached into her satchel and pulled out an ancient rusty saw.

Grack laughed and shook his head. There was no way he wanted to be enemies with Splendid Wren. She didn't come out much, but whenever she did, even if it was just to get a hot dog, it was like spotting a special rare bird. She was always sitting off by herself, looking at picture books and knitting. Grack had always wondered about her.

And he wasn't mad at Eggs either, not really. How could a girl who was not a bird but did bird stuff ever be chill and "grounded"? She couldn't even just hang out on the couch. Unless maybe it was a couch in a tree? Some kind of birdhouse or girl nest? A bed in the sky?!

Grack's clever mind was starting to have ideas.

"Flying girls!" he exclaimed.

"Flying girls," agreed Splendid Wren, with a sideways smirk and an extra-big shrug.

8

THE EGG FACTORY

Grack and Wren both later thought they miiiiight have noticed Eggs spying on them from the rooftops, but they couldn't be sure. So the next morning, when Grack brought Eggs to the roof of the abandoned carpet factory just around the corner, it was hard to tell if her delight was because she was surprised or because Splendid Wren was already hammering forklift pallets into a shape that kind of looked like a box.

Only a few hours of hammering, unhammering, and rehammering later, Wren had built a half-decent rectangular Eggs-sized coop, while Grack climbed down and up the dozen flights of rotten stairs like twenty times, lugging wood from the alley.

Eggs hopped about on top of the chimney, chirping about how much she loved Wren and Grack for being so sweet to her. She was 100 times more excited than a non-flying person would be, because hammers and forklift pallets were so heavy, and heavy stuff was just really not her thing. To Eggs, these two weren't just doing her a favour. They were doing the unthinkable impossible for her. Now Eggs would have her very own carton in which to ride out the winter.

That night, the three of them threw a nest-warming party, with Grack grilling non-stop every possible kind of hot dog. And Wren brought her enormous jug of homemade potent fruity flower juice. She said her juice was full of vitamins and energy. It had tiny flowers floating around in it and was super sweet. Wren claimed it didn't have any sugar, but all three of them still got all hyper and ran around the roof.

"Show me how to do that!" Splendid Wren squeaked when Eggs launched herself off her new rooftop, bounced off a metal catwalk, and fluttered up onto an old blank billboard.

Eggs looked deep in thought for a second. Like, really deep in thought. Then she said, "Flap up on top of that air conditioner," pointing to a big metal box on the roof, just a bit taller than Wren.

As an experiment, Wren tentatively jumped up and down, getting not even half as high as the air conditioner. She decided to climb up on top of it. Eggs and Grack watched her struggle, and then swing her feet up to get on top.

Wren stood up straight and proudly announced, "There!"

Eggs looked sideways at Grack. He couldn't tell, but he was pretty sure she winked at him.

"Now you are up one Wren high," said Eggs. "Launch yourself from there toward my egg carton and see how far you can get."

Wren flew about thirty centimetres forward, and then two metres straight down onto the asphalt roof. She then lost her footing, wiped out, and fell on her butt. Grack almost laughed, but then he concentrated really hard on not laughing and played it off cool.

"Okay," said Eggs. "Now do that again, but this time, don't *climb* onto the air conditioner, flap up there."

Splendid Fairy Wren closed her eyes and hopped up and down in place for a minute, seldom going higher than her own knees.

"Oh, whatever," Wren squeaked, kind of laugh-crying. The look on her splendid face showed that she was laughing because she was sad that her plan to do something impossible by just hoping that she could hadn't worked.

Grack took this as his cue that it was okay to laugh, too. But then Wren gave him a mean look.

"Eggs and I have hung out together for like a million hours." Grack shrugged into a smirk. "I've watched her jump off roofs and jump up onto roofs more times than anybody, and I still have no idea what she's doing."

"I'm flying," chirped Eggs with a grin. She jumped over a ledge and glided over the tip tops of half a dozen factory skylights.

Wren ran after her, daintily climbing up and down every kind of thing that might be found on a factory roof, chasing Eggs but with no thought of actually catching her. Grack followed—sort of off to the side—along normal stairs or the occasional ladder that he deemed acceptable. Carrying scrap wood up here all day was one thing, but he wasn't about to run through broken glass to roll in some tar on the roof. Plus, he was a cook, and cooks like stuff clean. He could appreciate the giant mechanical fan chimneys that the girls kept climbing as awe-inspiringly monstrous without getting un-wash-off-able robot juices all over his hands and semi-nice pants.

Wren and Grack got the workout of their lives chasing after Eggs as she pinged like a rubber ball from one otherworldly building to the next. After they climbed, or refused to climb, every single tower, turret, vent, shaft, elevator, water tank, skylight, and satellite dish, Eggs finally let them both collapse laughing in the big pile of old yarn and clothes they'd used to make her nest.

They all lay back and looked for stars, but it was so cloudy they only saw three. What they could see, from the carpet factory roof, was all kinds of dark shapes in the buildings. Little rectangles of sixty-watt amber light in every direction.

Just then, fifty Canada geese flew above them in one big honking, flapping formation. Eggs fluttered to the top of the tallest smokestack and honked back at them. Grack joked that they were probably all off to work the night shift at the pillow-stuffing factory. Wren giggled, her mouth full of chili dog and flower juice.

The three friends hung out all night long in Eggs's carton, wrapping themselves in sweaters and blankets and eating leftover hot dogs. They talked about a bunch of random stuff, and they all agreed that Eggs's new house was really great and hanging out together was pretty fun.

Eggs softened her skittish bird nature. She relaxed. She said all of them being friends was great 'cause they were all alike in this way that wasn't about flying or hot dogs or growing plants. Maybe it was about eating stuff on the roof—maybe that was it, that they all liked being on the roof together? Whatever it was, them being friends was really lucky and neat and great.

That late-fall nest-warming party, and how fantastically happy Eggs was, is both Grack and Wren's favourite memory. It was early winter, not even New Year's, when they lost her.

9

BORROWING STUFF

Despite a wandering life scavenging for leftovers and living outside on roofs, Eggs was a good-natured person even before she met Grack and Wren. Eggs refused to ever become a burglar or thief, as she disliked carrying any kind of bag or purse, or even having things in her pockets. Nobody is perfect, though, and because of her impulsive, airheaded, fluttery bird brain ... Eggs had one ... tiny ... persistently unmanageable personality flaw. She would borrow people's stuff without asking, and then forget to give it back.

As the threat of winter turned to the certainty of snow, Eggs would fly around keeping an eye out for coats and hoodies to wear for a few hours while resting and shivering on a phone pole. Then she'd ditch the jackets to fly off in search of adventures and snacks.

The cold snap had escalated so suddenly that, one night, there was freezing rain. Instead of fluttering into the city for a coat, Eggs took one off the roof of the nearby housing project. She lucked into a bright red jacket made of ultra-soft material that had been seemingly abandoned and forgotten, draped over the back of an aluminum and blue plastic lawn chair that looked like someone had set up for suntanning twenty degrees ago. She briefly wondered if the jacket had been there for weeks. Score!

And so it happened that Eggs was spotted perched on the phone lines above the auto body shop, slowly dirtying up the quite recognizable $400 golden-red silk bomber jacket of a local bad guy named Robin.

Robin was infamous in the neigh-bourhood. He was a semi-grown-up bully, always mean and always angry. He stole bikes, got in scary fights, sold pirated DVDs and video games, as well as these outlawed insane-o pills that tasted like jelly beans but had some weird chemical sugar that made whoever ate them go out-of-control hyperactive for three hours, barf, and then pass out wherever they stood. He was always trying to get people to eat them, even though they were kind of horrible.

He was the type of guy who walked up to people and stole the hot dogs right out of their hands, and then laughed at them while he ate it. The worst part? Lots of people thought he was a badass, cool bad guy. It made no sense, but it was still true.

Robin eventually got word that the weird girl had been seen climbing smokestacks and getting grime all over his jacket. He was super upset 'cause he wasn't about to let a crusty busker, or whatever she was, pull one over on him.

It was easy work to intimidate gutter punks. Eventually, Robin threatened to punch some dumb kid, who then tipped him off that the girl's name was maybe Eggs, and maybe she could be found in her winter hideout—a sort of pigeon coop that the hot dog guy and the sock-knitting girl had built for her on the roof of the abandoned carpet factory, just next to the big freight train yard.

10

EDGE-OF-THE-ROOF NIGHTMARE AT 100 FEET

Robin found Eggs up there in her carton on the roof at 10:59 p.m. She was bundled up, hiding cozily from the last of the freezing rain. Without even thinking—which wasn't really his kind of thing anyway—Robin started whacking Eggs repeatedly with a thin piece of lumber he found on the roof. The golden-red silk bomber jacket absorbed the worst of the blows, but it also got torn, ripped, and punctured. Robin was ruining his jacket way faster and worse than Eggs had.

Before Eggs could even blink herself awake, she was jolted by sharp multi-pointed pokes of pain from all the bent nails and screws in the board. She leapt out of the coat and, in one continuous, smooth motion, threw it over Robin's head. Robin stepped back—and realized he must have taken too many insane-o pills. He had a ridiculously hard time just trying to get the jacket off his head.

Meanwhile, Eggs kicked the main back wall of her pigeon coop hard, which caused the heavy forklift pallet roof to fall on Robin. He threw it off, too powered up on insane-o pills to care or properly notice that he got poked bad by a dozen nails in the wall's collapse. He furiously kicked her stupid house over and picked up a yard-long splintered pine board with several twisted nails curled around the edges.

Robin swung the board at Eggs, and she almost dodged it in a feat of wildly improvised trapeze-act-like tumbling. But then she registered that she had been cut painfully across her cheek. This was a good

time to be scared 'cause Robin was going all wild and out of control and screaming and lashing out at random. He had no plan but rage. If he got close enough, Eggs realized, then he might really hurt her.

Suddenly, Eggs fell back on a piece of hard, lumpy canvas. It was Wren's sack of hammers! With no time to think, she swung the sack at Robin, just to push him back, but it ripped open in motion and pelted him with a rain of mismatched old rusty tools. He fell down, yelling curses and screaming wild nonsense, while Eggs scrambled up the ledge of the closest factory wall.

It was the worst wall, too—the side of the factory next to the train yard. Below her was just ten storeys of window-less, balcony-less, ledge-less, nearly seamless limestone, and then miles of freight trains and locomotives, all swapping cars back and forth like a big dangerous robot worm fight.

Robin got up, wobbling goofily, waving his arms for fear of more hammers hitting him. But he found himself stuck to the spot! He tried and failed over and over again to lunge at Eggs. Robin realized he was looking really foolish trying to fight a not-very-big girl. Working extremely hard to force his brain to figure out what was going on, Robin located and then studied his foot. Nails! Somehow, between Robin kicking her house down and Eggs throwing a dozen hammers at him, his foot had gotten nailed to the roof.

Robin bellowed a wordless ARRRRRRGGGGG-HHHHH and grabbed for any wood scraps in reach,

throwing them in random directions, hoping to hit Eggs by chance.

Eggs sneered at him, clinging by just her toes to the roof's long ledge. She rose up, puffing herself up, and squawked mockingly at Robin. Then she scratched the ground definitively with her foot, spread her imaginary wings to their five-foot-eight grandeur, fluttered her long fingers, and dove off the side of the factory. She plummeted more than 100-something feet to the train tracks, with absolutely nothing at all to break her fall ...

11

IF EVERYONE HATES HIM, DOES HE TELL THE TRUTH

No one has seen or heard from Eggs in months. A bunch of punks talked big about throwing Robin off a roof, but no one did. He's still a bad, mean, criminal dumb guy, his only satisfaction being his new painful-looking limp that he actually seems kind of proud of. No one thinks he's cool anymore. His rep is completely trashed now.

Some negative people would try to convince you that Eggs dropped 100 feet right into a speeding junk train pulling 200 gondolas of twisted scrap steel, and any identifiable scrap of her went to the foundry, her soul now diluted among 1 million tons of construction rebar.

Grack, Splendid Wren, the hotel punks, and all the rest of us who can't bear to part with our very own folk hero can only find solace in the ranting mumbles of the loathsome jerk who chased her off a building.

According to Robin, fighting down an overpowering urge to throw up and pass out, he pulled the nails out of his foot and collapsed in agony at the edge of the roof, just in time to see Eggs still falling. Still falling ... though it had been a while, long enough, he thought, that she should have hit that speeding junk train by now.

She was falling horizontally, at the speed of a Frisbee, maybe riding the air current above the freight train, surfing on one of Wren's old hoodies that she'd been half-wearing under Robin's jacket to keep warm as she slept. She'd drifted down twenty feet, thirty feet, forty, fifty—and suddenly, she was also half a mile away. Then Eggs shook her arm out of the hoodie sleeve, shot up, caught some complex air pattern above a train and truck crossing, and was flung into a recessed highway.

Robin claims he saw her bounce off the roof of an eighteen-wheeler hauling chicken guts to the pet food factory. Then she bounced and rolled like a clumsy cartwheel onto the roof of another truck doing twice her speed and was thrown backward and forward at the same time.

She launched over the big green sign announcing the turnoff to the harbour. Then, she seemed to soar above the traffic before the road turned one way and Eggs just kept riding the air in a straight line. She cleared the top of a billboard advertising discount holiday flights, and then because of the downward curve of the highway, she was almost eighty feet up in the air again.

Just before she finally disappeared behind the billboard, she was flapping her arms as hard as she could, angled just slightly upward, eyes locked on the horizon, aimed toward the harbour with all the different boats and giant ships coming and going to who knows where in the world.

12

THE MOST LEAST REASONABLE THING

Grackle McCart and Splendid Wren spent the whole next week scouring Eggs's alleged flight path as best they could, though it meant searching train tracks and a truck highway and a container shipyard filled with mostly unhelpful, antagonistic, disbelieving security guards. They never found a ragged T-shirt or red jeggings or socks with holes or anything at all.

Grack said all this was proof she'd escaped. He said that regardless of whether she has any actual ability to fly, what is known for sure is that Eggs is impossibly, perhaps supernaturally, lucky at falling and has walked away from falls that high before.

But that just upset Wren. "Well, if she's okay, then why hasn't she come to us?! Wouldn't that be the most reasonable thing to do if a bad guy was after you?"

"Eggs has never had anything to do with reason." Grack went on using his smart-guy voice, "Therefore, the most reasonable thing to have happened to her is also the least reasonable."

"Oh, great," said Wren. "You probably made her go try to get a job at the pillow factory."

They both laughed. But then they walked up and down the train tracks for the seventh time, kicking rocks and looking for any kind of clue. Wren didn't know what to think. She just hoped Grack was right because he knew what he was talking about. Probably? Right? Right?

After a week of searching, Grack and Wren climbed to the roof of the carpet factory and nailed Eggs's little birdhouse back together, just in case.

Ever since then, Grack has been leaving bags of old hot dog buns up there. He hasn't seen Eggs, but every week, he finds the coop full of crumbs and all the bags torn open and eaten. Even though money is tight, and neither Wren nor Grack can offer a prize bigger than hot dogs or knit socks, they can guarantee that any information on her whereabouts will also be rewarded with fantastically wonderful Eggs.

Splendid Wren suspects Eggs must have gone south for the winter. She asks everyone she knows down there in attics and tall buildings to keep an eye on ledges, roofs, awnings, and thick phone wires. Wren recommends leaving brightly coloured food on ledges in open windows to try to catch Eggs long enough to convince her to take care of herself and do healthy things. And to please pass Eggs the message that whatever happened, her friends can't wait to see her again, whenever that is. And wherever Eggs is now, she's not alone.

ACKNOWLEDGMENTS

My gushing love for my forever partner in mostly totally legal crimes, CASEY PLETT. Not only would this book have stayed in a drawer forever without her and her weeks of editing and revising, but her ultra-deep understanding of complex, nuanced characters saw past my nonsense and nurtured furious rusty mangled heart laugh cry and love again.

To my genius artist little sister, Diddi, and my gang of nieces, Hails, Madeline, and Chelz, who give